PUFFIN BOOKS

More Television Adventures of S̶

'I'm Super Gran ... and I can do *anythi̶*

It was one of Mr Black's incredible ̶̶̶̶̶ wnich turned
Willard's frail little grandmother into the Super-charged Super
Gran – but not all his inventions have such a happy outcome.
Somehow that dastardly twosome the Scunner and Tub always
seem to get their hands on Mr Black's latest invention and put it to
use for their own evil little schemes. The chaos and confusion this
creates is hilarious and Super Gran often has a very tricky time
sorting it all out!

This new collection of stories is based on the hugely popular Tyne
Tees television series and will raise a chuckle from every young
reader.

Forrest Wilson

MORE TELEVISION ADVENTURES OF

SUPER GRAN

based on TV scripts by Jenny McDade and Forrest Wilson

Illustrated by David McKee

PUFFIN BOOKS

Puffin Books, Penguin Books Ltd, Harmondsworth, Middlesex, England
Viking Penguin Inc., 40 West 23rd Street, New York, New York 10010, U.S.A.
Penguin Books Australia Ltd, Ringwood, Victoria, Australia
Penguin Books Canada Ltd, 2801 John Street, Markham, Ontario, Canada L3R 1B4
Penguin Books (N.Z.) Ltd, 182–190 Wairau Road, Auckland 10, New Zealand

First published 1984

Made and printed in Great Britain by
Richard Clay (The Chaucer Press) Ltd,
Bungay, Suffolk
Filmset in Monophoto Photina by
Northumberland Press Ltd, Gateshead,
Tyne and Wear

Contents

Super Gran
and the Clocks

Mr Black sat in the passenger seat of his bubble car and mopped the bubbles of sweat from his forehead. He was supervising Super Gran as she drove, but her driving of the car – was driving him mad!

She jammed the brakes on at traffic lights, and shot him forward towards the windscreen.

'Is it absolutely necessary for you to learn to drive?' he asked. 'I mean, with all your Super-powers do you really need to?'

'But I *can* drive,' she explained. 'I told you, I just need some practice before I take my driving test. And just think, when I get my licence I'll be able to take my friends, the Oldies, out for wee hurls.'

'Hurls?'

'Aye. Wee hurls in a car. Outings.'

And with that the lights changed and she lurched the car forward again, shooting Mr Black back in his seat as she did so.

'Hey! Not so fast, Super Gran,' he yelled, as she shot off and weaved the car dangerously in and out of the traffic.

'But I'm used to zooming about everywhere. I don't like moving slowly.'

She wrenched the steering wheel this way and that and Mr Black was thrown this way and that in his seat.

'I'm really enjoying this, aren't you?' she grinned at him.

'N . . . no, n . . . not r . . . really,' he stuttered, terrified.

Suddenly she screeched the car to a halt – half a metre from the van in front of her! 'Och, scunners, it's another hold-up. And just as I was getting the hang of it, too!'

'What *is* the hold-up?' Mr Black asked presently, sticking his head out of the window. 'Looks like a traffic jam.'

'Traffic? T'rrific!' Super Gran giggled, as she dived out of the car. 'I'll go and see.'

She made her way past the long line of held-up traffic in the side street until she reached the main road, where she saw a flustered traffic warden, Tanya, trying to sort it all out.

'What's the matter?' she asked.

'Oh, just look at all this, Super Gran . . .' Tanya sighed.

She pointed to the dozens of vehicles which were congesting the road junction, spilling out of the side street on to the main road, so that none of them could move. 'What am I going to do with them?'

'Och, don't you worry, Tanya, I'll soon sort this lot out,' Super Gran assured her, with a grin. 'It's easy-peasy to someone Super like me!'

'But it's a complete jam-up. And none of the motorists'll move where I tell them to.'

'Leave it to me,' said Super Gran determinedly.

She went over to the car at the front of the line emerging from the side street, which was causing the jam. She asked the driver to move it back a couple of metres, having checked that there was room behind his car for him to do so. But he refused.

'Get lost!' he snarled. 'Who d'you think you are?'

She didn't argue, she merely went to the front of his car and, to his amazement, pushed it right back into the side street.

'That'll make some room,' she said, dusting off her hands as his car rolled backwards, away from the junction.

But Super Gran forgot how strong her Super-strength was. And she also forgot that the side street in which the line of cars was held up was hilly!

The driver, surprised at seeing a little old lady pushing his large, heavy car about, forgot to apply his brakes when it moved back too far! And it banged into the taxi behind him!

Then the taxi moved backwards down the hill and bumped into the car behind it, which ran back into the fourth vehicle, which ran into the fifth, in a sort of 'domino effect', so that each vehicle in turn collided with the one behind it, all along the line!

And the hill made the collisions all the easier, until the bumping eventually reached Mr Black's little bubble car.

'Yeeks!' he yelled.

He was helpless, in the passenger seat, to do much to avoid being hit by the car in front, or, in turn, bashing into the one at his rear.

'Well, Tanya, that's that lot sorted out.' Super Gran grinned cheerily, unaware of the chaos she had caused all the way down the line in the hilly side street.

'Thanks, Super Gran,' said Tanya gratefully. 'Oh, and did you hear the news?'

'News? What news?'

Tanya was excited. 'There's a TV company in town! One of their big vans passed me this morning while I was on point duty. Maybe I'll be discovered!' Her eyes sparkled.

For years Tanya had longed to be a star of stage, screen and pop music, and she was patiently waiting for some big TV or film producer to discover her and give her a chance.

'Just think, Super Gran, I could be a famous singer like

Dolly Barton, or a famous dancer or a famous actress ...'

'So you could, Tanya,' Super Gran said, waving good-bye to her.

But Super Gran knew that that wasn't too likely. For Tanya certainly sang like a bird – that is, she screeched like an owl! And she danced like a baby – a baby elephant!

As she walked back along the line towards Mr Black's car, she was so busy with her crazy thoughts of Tanya as a singer and dancer that she didn't notice that the cars were all bashed together. Nor did she notice the angry, fist-shaking drivers!

'Right, that's that lot sorted out,' she said as she jumped into the car again, 'so it's back to my driving lesson ...'

'Groans, must we?' Mr Black muttered, turning pale at the very idea. He still hadn't got over the shock of his car being sandwiched!

'What's happened here?' Super Gran asked, noticing for the first time that Mr Black's car seemed to be jammed tight between the one in front and the one behind. 'How did you end up like this? What on earth have you been playing at? I turn my back for a few minutes and ...'

'Of course you wouldn't have had anything to do with it, would you, Super Gran?' he sighed.

Meanwhile, the TV van – with CONVIX PIX painted on its side – which Tanya had seen was now parked outside the Scunner's house, while, inside, the Scunner was asking Tub what he thought of his latest disguise.

Munching a hamburger, Tub looked the Scunner up and down. He saw that he was wearing a wig, an imitation moustache, a pink open-necked shirt with a floral cravat, and dark sun-glasses, and that he had a fat unlit cigar in his mouth.

'What're you supposed to be, Uncle?'

'Isn't it obvious, Tub? I'm disguised as a big TV producer. All big TV producers look like this.'

'Yeah? But what's the idea?'

'I'm just about to pull off another job ...'

'Yeah?' Tub had another bite at his hamburger.

'I'm posing as that well-known TV producer, Herbert Hotchkick.'

'What – Herbert Hotchkick ... ?' echoed Police Inspector Muggins a short time later, as he read the name on the business card which the disguised Scunner presented to him in his office. 'So what can we do for a big, important, famous TV producer like you, sir?'

'I'd like to do some location filming in Chisleton,' the Scunner – alias Herbert Hotchkick – fibbed.

'That sounds exciting,' the Inspector replied. 'What sort of programme will it be – cops and robbers?'

Yes, thought the Scunner, but not so much cops – as robbers!

'And is this your assistant?' Inspector Muggins asked, gesturing towards the disguised Tub, who sat on the chair next to the Scunner and clutched a clapper-board in his hand.

Tub, also, wore a false moustache, but it annoyed him – it was ticklish!

'Yes, that's right. He's my assistant director. That's Tub . . . er . . . I mean, Mr Tubbington.'

The Scunner rose and went over to point at a large-scale map of Chisleton which was pinned to the wall.

'I'd like to do our filming here,' he said, 'at Big Ben's Clocke Shoppe.'

The Inspector joined him at the map. 'Ah, yes, the antique shop? M'mm, well . . . it's all priceless stuff, certainly, but, well, seeing that it's you I suppose it'll be all right to give you clearance to do your filming there.'

'Excellent, excellent!' said the Scunner – alias Herbert Hotchkick.

'The only problem is, the owner's away on holiday and the shop's shut up,' the Inspector went on. 'But don't worry – I'll arrange to borrow the keys and let you in.'

'Thanks a million, Inspector,' the Scunner gushed.

Then, as they drove away in the TV van, the Scunner said to Tub: 'We'll pretend to be filming, but all the time we'll be robbing the place!'

'Yeah, Uncle. Brilliant.'

But Tub wasn't so enthusiastic later, when the van pulled up outside Big Ben's Clocke Shoppe. 'Huh? You're robbing a mouldy old clock shop?'

'They might be mouldy and old, Tub,' the Scunner explained, 'but they're priceless antiques. And Ray Ling, the "fence", has promised me a fortune if I can nick a load of them.'

They jumped out of the van and were met at the shop door by Inspector Muggins, with a bunch of keys in his hand.

'Here you are, Mr Hotchkick,' he greeted him. 'I've opened the door for you.'

'Thank you, Inspector.'

'And Mr Hotchkick,' Muggins smiled, as the Scunner went into the shop, 'could I have your autograph?'

'Of course,' smiled the Scunner. It wasn't often that anyone – and especially a police inspector – wanted his autograph!

By now a small crowd was gathering, curious to see what was going on with the TV van. Willard and Edison were among them and Tanya, coming along on her beat, approached them.

'I told Super Gran there was a TV company in town,' she said. 'I was right, wasn't I?'

The disguised Tub was soon struggling out of the shop with an armful of valuable antique chiming clocks, on his way to the van. The Scunner, too high and mighty in his role of big TV producer to help him, was strutting around trying to look the part, with a script under his arm and a light-meter in his hand.

'Now's my big chance, here goes ...' said Tanya, as she stepped towards the Scunner. 'Excuse me, Mr Hotchkick ...'

'Yes?'

'I'm here to audition ...'

'Audition?' said the thunderstruck Scunner to the star-struck Tanya.

'Yes, I've always wanted to be in showbiz,' she said. 'To star on the telly or ...'

'But I've got nothing to do with the telly,' the Scunner said, truthfully – until Tub, passing with another load of clocks, nudged him. 'Oh ... er ... um ... I mean ... of course, I'm a big TV producer, aren't I. I forgot!'

'Yes, well I may look just like an ordinary traffic warden,' Tanya said, 'but I know I could be a big TV star.'

'Ah ... er ... well, unfortunately we're not auditioning today.'

'Aw ...' Tanya couldn't hide her disappointment.

'Why don't you come back tomorrow?' the Scunner suggested.

Tanya's face broke into a smile again. 'Tomorrow? Great!'

'When we'll be miles away!' the Scunner muttered under his breath to Tub, going back for another load.

'Hey, ordinary traffic warden!' someone yelled at Tanya from a passing car. 'You're wanted at the other side of town. Come on ...'

It was one of Tanya's colleagues who'd been sent to fetch her. She said good-bye to Willard and Edison and jumped into the car.

The Scunner meanwhile had turned to a puffing, panting, hardworking Tub and said: 'Get a move on! Ray Ling is waiting at Chisleton Ferry to pick up this little lot ...'

Suddenly a hand tugged at the Scunner's sleeve. He looked round and saw Willard.

'Are you really filming for the telly, mister?'

'Of course we are,' replied the disguised Scunner.

'Then where are the cameras, huh?' asked the suspicious Willard.

'Cameras? Oh ... er ... ah ... um ... you see, it's a ... um ... new technique. They're all hidden in the van.'

As Willard moved away, doubtfully, the Scunner muttered: 'Humph! Smart Alec kids!'

Willard changed his mind and approached the Scunner again, as he was fastening the van's tailboard, ready for a getaway.

'What's the name of this programme, huh?' he asked.

'Er ... um ... ah ... it's called ... er ... "Clocking Off" ...'

'Never heard of it,' Willard replied.

'It's a new one,' the Scunner assured him. 'It's coming out – in a short *time*.' He sniggered, then added: 'In fact, any *time* now!'

'But where are all the actors, huh?' Willard went on, looking around and seeing none.

'Look, kid, go play in the traffic, will you!' the Scunner snarled.

He and Tub climbed into the van and the Scunner started to drive it away. Then, as Inspector Muggins waved it through the crowd, the Scunner put his hand out of the window and handed him a business card.

'You wanted my autograph, Inspector,' he said. 'Tee hee!'

'Oh, thanks,' Muggins said. Then he looked at it. 'Hey! Wait a minute – it's the Scunner!' he yelled at the departing vehicle.

But over at the antique shop Willard was puzzled. The crowd was between him and Muggins and he hadn't seen him receiving the card.

'That was the funniest TV company I've ever seen,' he said.

'How many TV companies have you seen?' Edison asked.

'Well, actually, that was the first one,' he admitted. 'But what I mean is – where were all the actors? And where was all their gear – the cameras and lights and so on? Huh?'

'What was the company called?' Edison asked.

'Convix Pix,' he told her. 'I've never heard of them. I've heard of Tyne Tees and Thames and Central and . . .'

'Convix!' yelled Edison, as the penny dropped. 'Don't you see? Convix – convicts! They're crooks!'

'Crooks? And there were two of them,' Willard went on. 'And one of them was small and fat – just like Tub . . .'

'The Scunner!' Edison yelled.

'And they were robbing the place!' Willard added. 'I knew there was something funny about that TV van! I told you!'

'What'll we do?' Edison asked. 'That police inspector has run off somewhere and Super Gran's out in the car. She could be miles away, on the other side of town.'

'Unless we both shout for her – as loudly as we can,' suggested Willard.

Which they did.

And luckily Super Gran wasn't all that far away. She was still with Mr Black in his car and by now it was bumping its way across a piece of waste ground, littered with builders' rubble.

'I think you've taken a wrong turning somewhere,' Mr Black said as he mopped his brow for the umpteenth time. He resolved – if he survived this trip! – never to go out alone with her in a car again. It was nerve-racking!

'Wait a minute . .' she said as she screeched the car to a halt, almost sending him through the windscreen. 'I thought I heard something . . .'

She switched off the engine, and in the resulting silence tuned in her Super-hearing.

'Yes – it's a call for help. Sounded like Willard and Edison. Let's go.'

She started the car up again, slammed it into gear – and shot off, sending Mr Black backwards in his seat.

'Couldn't you go to them on foot?' he suggested. 'I know it would be slower – but it would be easier on my nerves!'

While Super Gran 'homed in' on the children's voices, the car zoomed out of the waste ground at about eighty miles an hour! It therefore took no time at all for them to reach the Big Ben Clocke Shoppe.

'What?' cried Super Gran. 'The Scunner and Tub! Robbing the shop?'

'Well, we think it might've been them.' Willard said, as he and Edison squeezed, somehow, into the back seat of the little car.

'But they could be anywhere by now,' Edison added as the car zoomed off once again.

Meanwhile, the Scunner was fairly drooling with pleasure over his morning's efforts.

'That was easy, wasn't it, Tub? In fact, to quote a certain enemy of mine, it was "easy-peasy"!'

'Yeah, Uncle.'

'Those clocks are worth thousands, you know,' he went on. 'And to think that they were pinched from right under the very noses of the police, too!' He laughed.

But, as the Convix Pix TV van zoomed along the road towards Chisleton Ferry, it was spotted – by the star-struck Tanya, who was now on point duty there.

'There's that TV van again,' she thought, and ran over to it when it stopped at the traffic lights.

'You won't forget my audition tomorrow, will you?' she smiled.

The Scunner leaned out of the van window. 'I've forgotten it already, Tanya – you tatty, talentless, traffic warden twit!'

Tanya's smile faded and, close to tears, she bit her lip. But just then part of the Scunner's disguise – his moustache and wig – fell off and landed at her feet!

'Hey! You're not a big TV producer,' she cried, 'you're a big Chisleton Scunner!'

'Yes, that's right, you meter maid menace!' he jeered, as the traffic started to move again. 'So if you'll excuse us, we must be off. We have a date at the ferry ...'

'Ferry nuff!' giggled Tub, as the van shot away again.

Meanwhile, the bubble car was also zooming along the ferry road.

'But how will you know where to find them?' Willard asked.

'Yes,' Edison added, 'and how did you know to come this way?'

'By using my Super-hearing power,' she explained.

'But how can you?' Edison asked. 'You can't possibly pick out the sound of their van from among all the other traffic noises.'

'No, that's true, but I'm tuning in to another sound.'

'What sound, Super Gran?' Mr Black asked.

'Well, tell me,' she said, 'what has the Scunner stolen, eh?'

'Clocks,' Willard replied.

'And what do some clocks do, every hour and half-hour,' she went on. 'And sometimes every quarter-hour?'

'They strike and chime . . .' said Edison.

'Exactly! So, just about now,' Super Gran went on, glancing at her watch, 'there should be a terrific din – when they all strike and chime at once!'

But Edison was still puzzled. 'Yes, but how did you know to come this way – when the clocks aren't striking yet?'

'I can Super-hear them all ticking,' Super Gran explained.

Meanwhile, as they drove along, the Scunner and Tub were being startled out of their cotton socks! For the dozens of antique timepieces in the back of the van started to strike and chime – all at once!

'Yeeks!' cried Tub, putting his hands over his ears.

'What the . . . ?' yelled the Scunner, looking round towards the noise behind him, and swerving the van on to a traffic island in fright!

'I hear them!' cried Super Gran to the others in the car. 'They're going this way . . .' And she swung the car round a corner in hot pursuit.

They whizzed along the road until they spotted Tanya, who waved them down.

'It's the Scunner! And he's heading towards the ferry,' she said. 'Is there room inside for one more?'

There wasn't! But that didn't stop her cramming herself in on top of the others!

'There they are!' yelled Willard presently, pointing ahead.

Super Gran put her foot right down on the accelerator until she overtook the van. Then she cut in front of it, and the Scunner had to swerve into the side of the road to avoid being hit.

Super Gran, Willard, Edison and Tanya scrambled out of the car and ran to confront the Scunner and Tub. But the Scunner managed to open his door and jump out before they got there.

Tub, however, being fatter and slower, couldn't escape before Tanya, Willard and Edison reached the van, slammed the doors shut and trapped him inside.

'I'll go after that scunnery Scunner,' Super Gran yelled, 'and you three can guard Tub.'

The Scunner, peeved at having to leave his 'swag' in the van, went racing off towards the ferry.

'I'll get you!' Super Gran promised, as she chased after him.

'Not if I reach the ferry, you won't,' he shouted back over his shoulder.

As he ran, a man stepped out in front of him and held up his hand. It was Ray Ling, the 'fence', who had been lounging against a railing fence, waiting for the Scunner and his 'swag'.

'Hey, stop, Scunner! Where are the timepieces you pinched for me?'

But the Scunner ran right past him. 'Can't stop, Ray ...

I haven't *time*. And if I stop – *I'll* get pinched!' He glanced back at Super Gran.

'*Timepieces?*' yelled Super Gran. 'When I catch him *he'll* get *time* – in jail! And *we'll* get *peace!*'

The ferry, a hundred metres away, was just leaving. But the Scunner put a spurt on, reached the pier and jumped aboard, clearing the two-metre gap which now gaped between the pier and the departing vessel. Then he turned to jeer at Super Gran, who hadn't got there in time.

But he jeered too soon. For she reached the pier and she jumped towards the ferry. And the fact that the gap was now about five metres didn't deter her. She cleared the gap as if she were stepping off the pavement!

'Huh?' said the Scunner, as Super Gran landed on the deck and threw herself at him, all in one movement.

'Gotcha!' she cried as she felled him.

Then, while he lay there dazed, she grabbed a chain from the side of the deck and wrapped him up in it!

Later, at police headquarters, she handed the Scunner and Tub over to Inspector Muggins, who said: 'Bah! Make a muggins of Muggins, would you, Scunner?'

Then he turned to Super Gran, smiled and thanked her.

'Och, don't mention it, Inspector,' she said. 'It was easy-peasy. I just zoomed along in Mr Black's wee bubble car and headed him off, that's all. Oh, and that reminds me,' she added, turning to Mr Black, 'talking about cars – when d'you think I'll be ready to take my driving test ... ?'

Mr Black turned pale and retorted: 'In about twenty years!'

'Humph! Cheek!' said Super Gran, all peeved, while Willard, Edison, Tanya and Inspector Muggins all laughed heartily.

'Och, well,' said Super Gran, relenting and joining in the laughter, 'maybe you're right at that!'

Super Gran
and the Magician

As Willard and Edison walked along the High Street they
wondered why a crowd had gathered outside the local
theatre, the Chisleton Empire, and what all the fuss was
about.

'What's going on over there?' Edison asked, pointing.

'Dunno. Let's find out,' said Willard as they crossed the
street to the Empire.

They joined the crowd, but neither of them noticed that
one of its members was – Tub.

On the theatre steps stood a magician. He was dressed in
his full outfit of white tie and tails and a swirling black cloak,
the way he was featured in a large photograph poster on the
theatre wall. He was billed as the Great Ronaldo.

'And now, ladies and gentlemen, boys and girls,' he said,
as he picked up his top hat, 'I shall attempt to produce – from
this empty hat – a real live rabbit . . .' He was giving a preview
of his act in the theatre that evening, and getting in a bit of
practice.

But the Great Ronaldo wasn't too successful. In fact, he
wasn't successful at all! He felt around inside the hat, smiling
as he did so. But his smile faded when he found nothing
there. He looked inside it. But he still found nothing. He
turned it upside down and shook it, but still there was no sign
of his furry friend. Willard, Edison and the rest of the crowd
laughed uproariously.

'Where's the rabbit? Where's Bugs Bunny?' yelled a man in the crowd.

'Yeah,' someone else shouted. "What's up, Doc?"'

'The Great Ronaldo doesn't look too great to me,' Willard muttered.

'He's just pretending to be hopeless so that everyone'll go to the theatre and see him do the tricks properly,' Edison suggested. 'If he's called the Great Ronaldo then he must be a top-class magician.'

But as the man lifted his props and went back into the theatre, Willard shrugged. 'I dunno.'

The crowd broke up and wandered off. But as Willard and Edison remained near the entrance, Tub also hung about, hiding behind a pillar to spy on them.

Willard pointed to the poster. 'That photo looks dead ancient. Maybe he was great then ...'

'But he's not much good now, is he?' Edison said.

Then she noticed that the theatre door was ajar. 'Come on, let's go in and have a look around ...'

Inside the theatre they opened a door and peeked in at the rows and rows of empty seats. In front of them, on the stage, stood the Great Ronaldo and his mother, Ivy. And behind them, although they didn't notice him, was Tub, who had followed them in!

While the Great Ronaldo – known to his friends as Ronald! – had been performing outside the theatre, Ivy had been awaiting his return on stage, where he would continue his last-minute practice.

'It's no use, Mum. I've had it. I'll never be the Great Ronaldo again.'

'Of course you will, Ron. You can do it. You can be great again,' she assured him. 'You used to be top of the bill.'

She sighed with pride as she glanced at the life-size photograph, like the poster outside the theatre, which stood at the side of the stage.

'But that was years ago, Mum. I've lost my touch – and my confidence. I'm *bottom* of the bill now!'

'But this is your big chance, Ron, your come-back. Once you're on stage tonight and the spotlight's on you, you'll be great again. The audience'll love you, I know they will. Now, have a go at your first trick again ...'

'OK, Mum.'

Ronald sighed and walked over to a large oblong box

covered in multi-coloured glitter which lay across a couple
of trestles. Inside it there was a wooden doll, its arms and legs
sticking out of holes at each end. He addressed the imaginary
audience, saying:

'Ladies and gentlemen, before your very eyes I shall now
attempt to saw this young lady . . . in half!'

Ivy cheered and applauded to encourage him.

He placed the saw in its groove in the centre of the box,
where the doll's waist would be, and began sawing like mad.
After a few minutes he had sawn right through the box and
he pushed the two separate halves away from each other.

But as he did so he stared with anguish at the doll. For it

too had been sawn in half and the sawdust gushed out on to the floor. He had failed again. As usual!

He burst into tears! 'It's no use!'

'There there, Ron,' said Ivy, patting his shoulder to comfort him.

'It's hopeless, Mum. If I can't perform the trick with an old wooden doll – how am I going to do it with a real live girl?'

'Yeah,' Edison whispered to Willard, at the back of the stalls, ''cos she wouldn't be a real live girl for long at that rate!'

She giggled and Willard sniggered and Ronald and Ivy looked down from the stage to see what was going on.

'Who's there?' Ronald asked nervously.

'It's only mice,' his mother said. 'You're just nervous.'

'But it's hopeless,' he repeated. 'I'm past it and there's no one can help me.'

'Someone can . . . !'

Edison had shouted out. She couldn't help herself. And she startled Ronald and his mother on the stage. 'I know the very person – Super Gran.'

'Who's Super Gran?' asked Ivy.

Willard and Edison, between them, explained all about her and how she could possibly help.

'We'll go and fetch her,' Willard offered, and he and Edison ran from the theatre.

But, once again, they didn't notice Tub hiding in the shadows.

Presently Super Gran arrived and asked: 'How can I help you?'

Ronald explained that he was no longer the great magician he had once been, years ago.

'What happened?' asked Super Gran.

'The Fabulous Finnegan happened,' he replied sadly.

'Who's the Fabulous Finnegan?'

'He was a flop, a failure, a third-rate conjuror. But he was jealous of my success ...'

'Tell them about the Houdini box, Ron,' his mother urged.

'Yes, well,' Ronald continued, 'I was checking out my special Houdini escape box one night, before the evening performance, when someone suddenly pushed me inside it, closed the lid, fastened the straps and padlocks and shot it down through the stage trapdoor ...'

He paused for breath while three pairs of ears gave him their whole attention.

'Go on,' Ivy nagged him.

'Then someone stuck labels on the box – and I was posted to the Hebrides! I was the laughing stock of the Magic Circle!'

'Yes,' Ivy added, 'but worse was to follow. For Finnegan took Ron's place that night at the performance.'

'And it was the beginning of his success,' Ronald went on. 'He stole my act, my props, my audience and my applause. Everything.'

'So it must've been Finnegan who sent Ron packing,' Ivy said.

Edison couldn't help giggling at Ivy's choice of the word 'packing'!

'That's a shame,' said Super Gran sympathetically.

'The whole thing undermined my confidence,' Ronald explained. 'And I've never worked since as a magician.'

'But this is his big chance,' Ivy went on. 'This is supposed to be his come-back performance tonight. Except that he can't even do the simplest trick properly. He's got no self-confidence – and he's a bundle of nerves.'

'Well,' said Super Gran thoughtfully, 'I don't really think my Super-powers could help you, but I'll have a wee think about it anyway.'

Meanwhile, Tub had quietly sneaked out of the theatre and was reporting what he had seen and heard to the Scunner.

'Super Gran's going to help Ron become the Great Ronaldo again,' he said.

'So the old pest is up to her do-a-good-deed-a-day nonsense again, is she?' the Scunner muttered. 'She's helping that crummy conjuror, is she? Then we'll "un-help" him!'

He laughed his nasty laugh as he hurried over to his phone and dialled a number.

'Who are you calling, Uncle?'

'I'm calling someone who'd like to keep the former Great Ronaldo from being great again ...' He spoke into the phone: 'Hello, is that the Fabulous Finnegan?'

Back at the theatre, in the wings, Super Gran and company watched Ronald practising another trick on stage.

He stood beside his upright 'vanishing' cabinet, covered with the usual multi-coloured glitter, and addressed his imaginary audience: 'Ladies and gentlemen, I shall now attempt my most difficult trick – making someone disappear.' He then turned to the woman from the audience who had volunteered to come on to the stage to help him. 'I have never met you before, have I, madam?' he asked, as he placed her in the cabinet.

'No, son ...' said Ivy.

'Mum!' he yelled in exasperation. 'You're supposed to be a stranger!'

'Sorry, Ron,' Ivy apologized, as her son slammed the door shut.

'Disappear!' Ronald commanded, as he whirled the cabinet round.

When it stopped he smiled in triumph and opened it. But his face fell, for Ivy was still there in full view. She hadn't disappeared – and he had failed again.

'Oh no!' he sighed wearily, looking towards Super Gran and the others in the wings. He shrugged. 'See what I mean?'

'Can't you do something to help him, Super Gran?' Ivy asked, stepping out of the cabinet. 'His performance starts in an hour.'

Super Gran turned to Edison and whispered: 'Your Grandad's Hypnotizer might do the trick, lassie. We could hypnotize him and tell him he's the Great Ronaldo again.'

'Yes, that might work,' Edison agreed.

'Could you fetch it, in a hurry?' Super Gran asked.

'OK,' said Edison, 'but I'll have to look for it. I don't know where he keeps it . . .' And she rushed out of the theatre.

Meanwhile the Scunner was getting dressed up, ready for a big night out.

'I managed to get tickets for seats in the front row of the stalls,' he said.

'But what are we going there for?' asked Tub, whose idea of fun was not a night at the theatre.

'We're going because I want to see the Great Ronaldo meet his Waterloo,' the Scunner explained.

'Waterloo?' gasped Tub. 'I thought it was the Chisleton theatre we were going to – not a London railway station!'

'A London railway station is where the Great Ronaldo will be ending up – or rather, will be starting out from! – when the Fabulous Finnegan gets to work on him again,' he said, laughing his nasty laugh.

Back at the theatre, in the dressing-room, a shaking, quaking Ronald was preparing for his come-back appearance on stage.

'B-but M-mum ...' he stuttered, 'I'm s-s-scared. I j-just c-can't go on. My kn-kn-knees are like j-j-jelly ...!'

'You've got to go on, Ron. This is your big chance and it might be the only one you'll get to make a come-back. And remember the old showbiz saying – the show must go on!'

'B-but Mum, I'm n-not s-stopping the sh-show going on. It c-can go on without m-me!'

There was a knock at the door, it opened and Super Gran stuck her head into the room.

'Dinna fear, Super Gran's here ...' she grinned. 'All your troubles'll soon be over.'

'Why – has the show been cancelled?' said Ronald, brightening.

'No,' she laughed, 'but I've got a wee gadget that'll hypnotize you and give you your confidence back.'

She looked out into the corridor. 'At least, I haven't got it yet, but Edison's bringing it. Isn't she here yet, Willie?'

Willard, waiting in the corridor, nodded. 'Yeah, here she comes. But I just hope she doesn't trip. She's always tripping when she's in a hurry ...'

They all heard the sound of Edison's footsteps as she raced along the theatre corridor towards the dressing-room, carrying the Hypnotizer. And they all heard the 'Ouch!' she yelled as she tripped – as usual!

Willard, in the corridor, made a valiant attempt at catching the gadget as it flew out of Edison's hands. But it went flying too high, over his outstretched hands.

'Oh no ... !' he yelled, as it hit the floor behind him.

He picked it up, shook it and handed it to Super Gran at the dressing-room door. 'Is it broken?'

'No, it's all right,' she said, after inspecting it. 'It's still working OK.'

Meanwhile, the Fabulous Finnegan had arrived at the theatre. He grinned up at Ronald's poster then hurried round to the side, to the stage door. He waited until the doorkeeper turned his back and then sneaked past him and down a stairway which led to the basement, under the stage. He took some large sticky labels out of his pocket and looked around for Ronald's Houdini box. As he spotted it he chuckled quietly to himself. And then waited.

Back in the dressing-room Super Gran pointed the Hypnotizer at Ronald. 'You are no longer plain Ronald,' she said. 'You are the Great Ronaldo once more. Do you understand?'

'Yes, I understand,' Ronald droned, in a trance-like voice.

'Then repeat after me,' Super Gran went on, 'there is no magician as great as the Great Ronaldo ...'

'There is no magician as great as the Great Ronaldo,' he repeated.

He left the dressing-room so full of confidence that he thought he was walking on air! Super Gran and the others followed him to the wings, where they all waited for the compère to make his introductions.

'And now, ladies and gentlemen,' the man said, 'the Chisleton Empire proudly presents – the Great Ronaldo!'

But while Ronald was making his entrance, dirty work was afoot beneath his feet! For, below stage, the Fabulous Finnegan, more interested in dirty tricks than magic tricks, was just about to give a repeat performance of the one he had played on Ronald previously.

He looked up towards the stage as he put his hand on a lever. 'So you and Ivy are trying to be stars again, are you? Well, instead of *being* stars, you'll be *seeing* stars – any moment now!'

Ivy, who was going to appear on stage as Ronald's assistant, instead of as a 'volunteer' from the audience, was now being put into the 'vanishing' cabinet.

Ronald turned to the audience: 'I shall now attempt to make my assistant disappear . . .'

But just then the Fabulous Finnegan pulled the lever. The trapdoor opened and Ronald shot through it and travelled on the little lift – which operated when the door opened – to the basement floor.

'Hey!' yelled a man in the audience, 'your assistant's supposed to disappear, not you!'

The audience roared with laughter at the Great Ronaldo's second-rate act, while Ronald, sitting dazed on the basement floor, looked up and saw –

'Finnegan . . . !'

'Hello, Ronnie. Trying to make a come-back, are you? You'll never do it!'

The Houdini box was all ready – with labels attached! – to receive the stunned Ronald. But Finnegan had reckoned without Super Gran!

For as soon as Ronald had shot through the trapdoor she had dived towards the little spiral staircase which led from the wings into the basement, below the stage. She raced down it to see if he was hurt and needed help.

But she stopped, halfway down the stairs, on seeing Finnegan about to push Ronald into the Houdini box.

'Hey, you wee bachle . . . !' she cried.

'Huh?' he exclaimed, looking up at her in surprise.

'I take it you're the Fabulous Finnegan?' she said. 'Well –
I'm the famous Super Gran!'

'I don't care who you are – you can wave your friend
Ronnie good-bye. He's going off touring again!' he laughed.

But before Finnegan could shove the stunned Ronald into
the box Super Gran threw herself off the staircase and landed
on the lever. Her weight pushed it down and the trapdoor lift
shot back up to the stage again, taking Ronald with it.

'Up you go, Ron!' she cried.

'Huh?' Ronald exclaimed. And:

'Huh?' Finnegan echoed. His plans had been thwarted.

Ronald stood on the stage once more, feeling like a yo-yo!

And Ivy, inside the box, wondered what on earth was going on out there!

'Ron, what are you playing at?' her muffled voice asked.

'Hey! I see you've come up in the world again!' The joker in the audience laughed loudly and everyone else joined in.

Meanwhile, below stage, Finnegan, having decided to tackle Super Gran, rushed across the floor towards her, his fists raised.

'Och, you wouldn't hit a poor, defenceless little old lady, would you?' she smiled, as she side-stepped and dodged him.

As he went past her she gave him a gentle karate chop to the side of the head. Not too hard, but just enough to stun him slightly. Then as he sagged at the knees she grabbed him, pushed him into the open Houdini box and closed the lid. She then pulled the trapdoor lever, brought the lift down, put the box on it and sent it up again.

Ronald was in the middle of another unsuccessful trick when the Houdini box suddenly appeared on the stage beside him. Super Gran thought that this might help his act, but her plan backfired.

In the first place the audience howled with laughter, thinking it was something else that had gone wrong with Ronald's performance. And secondly, the Fabulous Finnegan revived sooner than Super Gran had expected!

Finnegan lifted the lid of the box and looked out, to the delight of the audience, who roared with laughter! Then he climbed out and approached Ronald threateningly, his fists raised. He wasn't going to be made a fool of by him or his little old lady friend – and he intended doing what he had come there to do, audience or no audience! He was out to get Ronald!

'Who's that, Uncle?' asked Tub.

'That's the Fabulous Finnegan,' replied the Scunner. 'And he's here to get rid of that so-called Great Ronaldo. He's going to post him again – but this time to the farthest point in Britain!' He laughed nastily.

But Super Gran, in the basement, hearing the commotion on stage, quickly brought the lift down and rode up on it.

She reached the stage and Finnegan, turning away from Ronald, faced her instead. He clenched his fists and prepared to tackle her again.

But this time he didn't go near her. They circled around each other like two TV wrestlers looking for an opening.

And the audience yelled their encouragement! Their conjuring act had suddenly turned into a fight! They were certainly getting their money's worth!

Out of the corner of her eye Super Gran got a glimpse of the Scunner and Tub sitting in the front row of the stalls.

'Ah-ha, so *they're* here!' she murmured to herself. 'Well, all the better!'

She moved round until she was facing the audience, forcing Finnegan to turn so that his back was now to the audience. Then, judging him to be about level with the Scunner and Tub, she blew her Super-breath at him. The Super-blast knocked him off his feet, and off the stage – to land right on top of the Scunner and Tub! Her aim had been perfect!

'Great! Three birds with one stone,' she murmured. 'Or rather, three rats with one blow!'

Then, before Finnegan could recover from the shock of being blown off the stage by a little old lady, or recover from his bruises, Super Gran leapt off the stage, hoisted him on to her shoulder and climbed back on again.

'I'll take him off your hands, Scunner,' she laughed, as she lifted Finnegan.

'Ow! Ouch! Ooyah!' yelled the flattened Scunner and Tub.

She dumped Finnegan – not feeling so fabulous now! – unceremoniously into the Houdini box. Then Ronald leapt forward, to strap and padlock it, securing Finnegan inside.

'I've waited a long time to do that!' he said with a grin. 'Revenge is sweet.'

'Aye, and he can cool his heels in there for a wee while,' Super Gran said, 'while you carry on with your act in peace!'

She left the stage and dragged the Finnegan-filled Houdini box into the wings – to the wild applause of the audience! After which she, Willard and Edison joined them to watch the rest of the show.

And from then on there was no stopping Ronald. He was absolutely superb. The rest of his act was a huge success and it was clear that he would very soon be the Great Ronaldo once again.

Afterwards, in the dressing-room, he thanked Super Gran for giving him his confidence back with the Hypnotizer.

'Och, but I didn't,' she confessed. 'When Edison dropped it, it really did break. I just pretended to hypnotize you ...'

'What?' he exclaimed. 'But I felt confident when I went on stage, so it must've worked.'

'No, you just told yourself it had worked. You weren't really hypnotized at all,' she said. 'And you didn't regain your confidence properly until you'd got your own back on Finnegan, by doing to him what he'd done to you – shoving him into the Houdini box and locking him in. I'm sure that's what did it.'

'Oh, Super Gran, we can't thank you enough for helping

Ron make his come-back,' said Ivy, giving Super Gran a big hug.

'Aye, and talking about the former Fabulous Finnegan,' Super Gran frowned, 'what happened to him?'

'Well, the last *I* saw of him,' Ronald said, 'he was firmly secured inside my Houdini box . . .'

'Aye, and I left it in the wings,' Super Gran added.

'Oh-oh!' muttered Edison.

'What is it, lassie?'

'Well, when we went down into the audience, I glanced back and saw the stage-doorkeeper dragging the box away from the wings. I never thought anything about it at the time . . .'

'Yeah,' Willard added, 'and it had labels stuck on it!'

'Don't tell me,' said Super Gran, horrified, 'that Finnegan's ended up in Fingal's Cave or somewhere!'

They all rushed out of the dressing-room and along to the stage door. But they were too late!

'It was marked "urgent", so I sent it off,' the doorkeeper told them.

'Not to the Hebrides?' Ivy gasped.

'No, to the Shetlands!' he replied.

'Jings!' Super Gran exclaimed, 'that's even farther away!'

'Oh well,' Edison said, 'one *bad* turn deserves another, huh?'

'Aye,' Super Gran agreed. She grinned and turned to Ronald: 'And just think – that's the best disappearing act you've ever done!'

Super Gran
and the Golfers

Super Gran was zooming all over Chisleton golf course on a
motorized lawn-mower, cutting the grass. She was supposed
to be helping the greenkeeper – but she was terrorizing
every golfer in sight! She hadn't quite got the hang of it yet!

'Look out!' she yelled.

'Look out, yourself!' yelled the golfers, running for their
lives from the middle of the fairway. 'Have you got a licence
to drive that?'

Three of the golfers in particular were annoyed at her antics and shook their fists at her. They were old, red-nosed, white-haired gentlemen who looked like retired army colonels.

The first one looked like a grumpy old meanie, the second one looked as if he was one of the 'horsey' set and the third one kept yelling at her: 'Mow over there, mow over there!', meaning any part of the golf course they weren't playing on. So she christened them 'Eeny-Meanie', 'My-Nay' and 'Mo'!

'Och, I'm away. Cheerio!' she said, giving them a cheery wave and zooming the mower off in another direction.

It was then she encountered Joe, who was a beginner at golf. In fact some joker had even fastened a car's L-plate to the back of his shirt and another one to his driver, which said: 'This is an "L" driver!'

He was trying to tee off and he wasn't succeeding! He swung his club at the ball three or four times and each time he swung himself off his feet. And when he finally managed to hit the ball, he kept losing it – and losing his temper. In disgust he went to break the club over his knee. But:

'Ooyah!' he yelled – for it was steel-shafted and was a lot tougher than his knee was!

That did it! That was the last straw! He'd had enough of golf! He would take up another sport instead!

He took the driver and, striding purposefully to the top of a nearby hill, he whirled it around his head and threw it as far as he could – straight into a river which meandered through the golf course at the foot of the hill.

'Good riddance!' he muttered, dusting off his hands.

He was now going to fetch the rest of his clubs – and the bag too – and throw the lot into the river!

But Super Gran came over the crest of the hill on the

mower just as his driver went flying into the water – and she thought it had just slipped accidentally!

'Never fear, Super Gran's here!'

She jumped off the machine, raced down to the river, grabbed a fallen tree-branch, hooked the club and pulled it out.

'There you are, laddie,' she said, all pleased with herself.

'Oh ... ah ... well ... you see ...' stuttered Joe, not quite knowing how to confess to her that he had thrown it in deliberately.

But he didn't need to! She read his mind!

'Oh, so you're giving up golf, are you?' she grinned.

'I'm hopeless,' he admitted. 'And I keep losing golf balls. It's costing me a small fortune! I've lost about fifty already – and I only took up golf yesterday!'

'Jings!'

'You see,' he explained, 'I take up a different sport every month. Last month it was jogging. The month before it was yoga.'

Just then Willard and Edison appeared over the hill. They were caddying for two prosperous-looking businessmen who each had expensive-looking golf trolleys which held large, expensive-looking golf bags containing dozens of expensive-looking golf clubs.

Willard was pulling his trolley but Edison had hers in front of her, pushing it – which was a mistake, on a steep hill with a river at the bottom!

'What you need,' Super Gran told Joe, 'is to tie a bit of string to your ball so that you won't lose it. In fact,' she added with a laugh, 'you'd be better with a piece of elastic. That way, the ball would keep coming back to you every time you hit it! You'd never lose it!'

While she and Joe were laughing at the idea of an elastic-assisted golf ball, Edison interrupted:

'My Grandad's got the very thing! It's a golf ball with a little radio transmitter inside it. It bleeps when it's hit and you can't lose it.'

'That sounds like a good idea,' Super Gran admitted. 'What do you think, Joe?'

Edison went on to explain: 'All you've got to do is follow the sound of the bleeps on a receiver. I'm telling you, you'll never lose a golf ball again. Shall I go home and fetch it?'

'Aye, lassie, why not?'

So Edison ran off. But she forgot she was supposed to be holding the handle of the golf trolley – and she let it go!

'Yeeks!' she yelled, as it zoomed down the steep hill towards the river at the bottom.

But if Edison yelled, the trolley's owner yelled even louder!

'Ye gods! My trolley! My golf bag! My clubs! Save them! They're worth hundreds! They'll be ruined!'

'I'll get it!' Super Gran shouted, as she sped down the hill after it.

She caught the trolley as it was about to plunge into the water and when its wheels were actually over the edge of the riverbank, suspended in mid-air!

And while this was going on, and the golfer's attention was firmly on Super Gran's exploits at the river's edge, Edison took the chance to sneak off home for the radio-controlled golf ball.

Having handed the trolley back to its owner, Super Gran left him, his partner, Willard and Joe to get on with her mowing.

Presently, as she drove the mower across the golf course,

she remarked: 'Jings! This grass is gey long. It's fairly need-
ing to be cut!'

'Madam!' a colonel-type voice barked at her. 'It's supposed
to be long here!' It was Eenie-Meanie.

'Humph! This is the "rough", don'tya know!' snorted My-
Nay.

'You mean, it *was* the "rough",' whined Mo. 'Just look at
it now. It's as smooth as a putting green!'

As Super Gran drove the mower away, she glanced back
and saw that the area which was supposed to have long,
rough grass was now indeed rather smooth. She also saw
Eenie-Meanie and My-Nay throwing their golfing caps on
the ground and jumping on them, in a temper. While Mo,
who didn't wear a cap over his thick, bushy white hair,
contented himself with pulling a handful of it out, to show
the other two that he was as angry as they were!

'Och, well, how was I supposed to know?' Super Gran said
with a smile. 'I don't know anything about golf!'

Meanwhile, a mile away, the Scunner was in his house
speaking on his phone. Tub stood beside him, eating a
jammy sandwich.

'Hello, lads,' said the Scunner over a crackling line. 'Did
you pinch the diamonds OK?'

'Yeah, we got two bags of them,' one of the Renta-Muscles
replied, from a phone box near Chisleton Common. 'But
we've gotta problem – a police road-block.'

He and his mate looked out of the box at the policemen
who were stopping and searching every vehicle which
passed along the main road. At the side of the box, on the
common, a number of boys were playing with radio-
controlled model aeroplanes.

'Where are you?' the Scunner asked.

'Common!' the Renta-Muscle replied.

'What d'you mean "common"?' the Scunner snarled. 'Who's common? You're one to talk about being common ...!'

'No, boss,' the man interrupted, 'Chisleton Common.'

'Oh ... ah ... the line's bad,' the Scunner said, making that the excuse for the misunderstanding. 'Isn't there a model aeroplane contest going on there today?'

'Yeah, looks like it.'

'I thought so,' said the Scunner. 'Then here's what to do ...'

The two Renta-Muscles left the phone box and went over to speak to the nearest boy. Well, not so much 'speak to him' as threaten him with violence if he didn't cooperate!

The noise of the dozens of planes zooming around overhead made it difficult for the boy to catch what the Renta-Muscle was saying to him.

'Blah ... blah ... blah ... DUFF ...' the Renta-Muscle said.

'What? It's *not* duff,' the boy denied indignantly. 'My plane's one of the best!'

'Blah ... blah ... blah ... DUFF ...' the Renta-Muscle repeated.

'What? *Plum* duff?' said the boy, shouting above the noise. 'What's plum duff got to do with model planes?'

The Renta-Muscle tried once more, thrusting his fist under the boy's nose, so that there was no misunderstanding this time!

'Blah ... blah ... blah ... *this* kinda duff – we'll duff you up!'

The boy got the message and the Renta-Muscles got the plane! As far as the boy was concerned it was either plane – or pain!

He helped them tie the first bag of diamonds on to the plane's undercarriage, so that it could be released on a signal from his controls. But the plane couldn't take the second bag of diamonds.

'It'll make it too heavy,' he explained, 'and the plane'll come crashing down.'

'So what'll we do?' the Renta-Muscle asked, a puzzled frown creasing his forehead.

'Make two trips!'

'Good idea, son,' the Renta-Muscle grinned.

The model plane took off, climbed into the sky over the common, over the main road – and over the heads of the unsuspecting policemen at their road-block.

'And when it gets back,' the boy said, 'we'll put the other bag on it. OK?'

The Scunner, meantime, was dashing from his house, followed by Tub, to go and look out for the plane when it made its drop. He had told the Renta-Muscles to drop the diamonds out in the country, rather than in town, in case someone saw them landing or, worse still, got the diamonds before he did!

'Come on, Tub, hurry,' he shouted over his shoulder as they headed out of town.

Meanwhile, Edison was also heading out of town, returning to the golf course with the bleeping golf ball and its receiver, which was the size of a small transistor radio.

She arrived at the course and contacted Super Gran. Then the two of them contacted Joe. But the learner golfer, who had removed his L-plates, merely shook his head.

'No thanks,' he said. 'I've definitely given up golf. I'm taking up snooker instead, for this month's sport. When you pot a snooker ball you've only got to walk round the table and lift it out of a pocket. You don't have to tramp all over Chisleton looking for it.'

'Aye, that's true,' Super Gran admitted with a smile.

'Here!' He thrust his bag of golf clubs at her and marched off. 'Take them. You're welcome!'

Just then Willard joined them. He had finished his stint as a caddy, had received his pay and was on his way into town to spend it when he spotted them.

'What're you going to do with *them*, Gran?' he asked, pointing to the golf clubs.

Super Gran had a gleam in her eye. 'Well, seeing that Edison has gone to the bother of fetching her bleeping ball...' – it sounded as if she were swearing! – '... and seeing

I've fallen heir to Joe's clubs – I might as well have a wee go and see if the ball works.'

'Of course it'll work,' said Edison indignantly.

'There's no point in letting a good invention go to waste, is there?' Super Gran added.

'Huh!' snorted Willard. 'Who says it's a good invention?'

'It is. You'll see!' Edison insisted.

But Super Gran wasn't listening to the argument. She was over at the first tee and was driving off.

The ball hit a tree, bounced off and hit another four trees in rapid succession. But as the trees stood facing one another at each side of the fairway, the heads of Super Gran and company had to move from side to side, like Wimbledon tennis spectators, to watch the ball go!

The ball then rebounded off the last tree and hit the clubhouse window. It smashed through it, passed through the bar – just missing the noses of Eenie-Meanie, My-Nay and Mo who were having drinks at the time – and out through the window at the opposite side!

'Grrr! Gnash, gnash!' went Eenie-Meanie and My-Nay, as they spluttered into their whiskies about the passing ball – while Mo yanked out another handful of hair.

But the ball's travels weren't over yet!

It came out of the window and hit a golf buggy, bounced off it, hit the top of the flag-pin on the eighteenth green – and slid down it!

'Wow! A hole in one!' exclaimed Edison, when they ran over and picked it out.

'No it's not,' Willard corrected her, 'it's a *round* in one! From the first tee to the eighteenth hole!'

But Super Gran was disappointed! 'Scunners!' she muttered.

'What?' Willard exclaimed. 'You couldn't possibly do a round in less than one shot! No one could!'

'Aye, but the idea was for us to lose the ball, so that we could find it with its bleeping device. But it's not lost if it's in the hole, is it? Anyone could find it there! I'll just have to have another shot, that's all!'

This time she really clobbered it. In fact, she Super-clobbered it the entire length of the course, and more! It went soaring up in the air and right out of the course – and landed in the Scunner's pocket!

The Scunner and Tub had been hurrying along the road, their eyes looking skywards for a sign of the approaching model aeroplane.

'There it is!' cried Tub, pointing.

They stopped running and positioned themselves under it to catch the bag of swag as it was released from the plane. It circled overhead, dropped the diamonds, then turned and flew back towards the common for its second load.

But the Scunner was so busy grabbing the bag, checking its contents and stuffing it into his right-hand pocket, that he didn't notice the golf ball plopping out of the sky into his left-hand pocket!

He rubbed his hands together gleefully, while Tub, a trifle disappointed, asked:

'Is that all they pinched? Just the one bag?'

'I'm not sure, I couldn't hear properly. It was a bad line. But don't worry, there's a fortune in that bag, I can assure you.'

'I'm famished, with all that rushing about,' Tub moaned, rubbing his empty stomach.

'I'll tell you what, Tubbo, my boy,' the Scunner said, with

a huge, diamond-studded smile, 'I'll stand you a meal in the Golf Café, how's about that, then?'

'Right! You're on!' said Tub, climbing over the fence into the golf course. 'We'll take the short cut!' He couldn't wait to get there!

The Scunner shrugged and climbed over the fence after him.

Presently, about halfway across the course, they spotted Super Gran and company in the distance, looking as if they were searching for something. Edison had a sort of transistor radio in her hands, while Super Gran and Willard kept poking around in the rough, in holes in trees and even in birds' nests!

Willard was even checking the hole in one of the greens!

'What the devil are you playing at?' barked Eenie-Meanie, as the boy lifted the three balls which he and his friends My-Nay and Mo had just newly putted in!

'They should be horse-whipped,' raged the horsey My-Nay, while Mo contented himself with a few 'Grrrrs!' and 'Gnash, gnashes' and some more hair-pulling!

But then Edison noticed that when she pointed the radio receiver in a certain direction its needle went berserk as it picked up the bleeps, indicating that the lost ball was somewhere that way. And she noticed, too, that the Scunner and Tub were in that direction, walking across the course in the distance.

She shouted to Super Gran, who was at that moment halfway up an oak tree, searching!

'Super Gran! It's over there! Look! The Scunner!'

They set off towards them and the bleeping got louder. It looked as if the Scunner had the ball – but how could he have?

'They're coming this way, Uncle,' said Tub, pointing.

'So I see. I wonder what they're after?' He began walking a little bit faster – just in case!

'Hey! Stop, Scunner!' Super Gran yelled.

'No fear!' he replied, walking even faster.

'You've got something . . .' Super Gran went on, as she and the others walked faster too.

The Scunner was forced to start running. 'Come on, Tub – they must've found out about the diamonds! They're after 'em! Run!'

'I wish . . . we had . . . some transport,' Tub moaned, as he puffed and panted behind the Scunner.

'Transport?' murmured his uncle, pointing. 'There's the very thing, Tub. Come on ...'

It was a motorized golf buggy which its owner had parked at the side of a green. The Scunner and Tub raced towards it, jumped aboard and zoomed off in it, while the golfer danced a jig of fury.

They whizzed the buggy up and down the hills and slopes of the golf course, and while the Scunner drove the vehicle, Tub looked back and thumbed his nose at Super Gran, who was chasing after it.

'Oh-oh,' he said.

'What is it, Tub?' asked the Scunner, concentrating on his driving.

'*She's* found one too!'

'If you can't beat them, join them,' said Super Gran as she spotted a second buggy and ran to 'borrow' it. 'Come on, kids,' she yelled to them over her shoulder. Then:

'Give it back, Scunner!' she shouted, as she and the children gave chase in the buggy.

The Scunner, of course, thought she meant the bag of diamonds, whereas she was only referring to the bleeping golf ball!

'Duck!' yelled Willard, as three golf balls suddenly came whizzing out of nowhere at them from different directions.

It was Eenie-Meanie, My-Nay and Mo again!

'Confound it, madam,' Eenie-Meanie said, as their buggy approached him and he had to jump out of its way. 'You're a positive menace on this course.'

'Of *course* she is!' agreed My-Nay, not realizing he had made a little joke.

'Grrr!' Mo gnashed his teeth and pulled out some more of

his hair, which was beginning to look positively sparse in places! 'We'll report you to the club secretary!'

The buggy hit a bump in the ground and Super Gran momentarily lost control of it. It curved round in a semi-circle – and headed straight for Eenie-Meanie, My-Nay and Mo again, and again they had to jump for their lives!

'Bah! Women drivers!' fumed Eenie-Meanie.

'The only drivers that should be allowed on a golf course are the ones you drive the ball with,' raged My-Nay, shaking his driver furiously to illustrate the point.

Super Gran glanced over at Mo to see what he was going to say. But he was too busy pulling out the last handfuls of his hair!

'Hey, Mo,' she laughed, 'you could do with mohair. With *mo' hair*!' She straightened the buggy up and set off after the Scunner and Tub again.

They bowled along the course, almost hitting other golfers as they went. Then, just as they caught sight of the Scunner and Tub, they saw that Tub was looking upwards, having spotted the model plane again.

'Look, Uncle,' he said, pointing, 'it looks as if it's going to make another drop!'

'What's that, Tub . . . ?'

The Scunner also looked upwards as the plane circled overhead – which was a mistake! He took his attention off his driving and the buggy toppled into a bunker. The two of them were thrown out and went rolling down the hill – and into the river at the bottom!

'Help! Splutter!' they yelled, as Super Gran zoomed to their rescue.

She jumped off the buggy, ran to the river, plunged in, grabbed them by their collars and yanked them out.

'Now,' she said, putting her hand into the Scunner's left-hand pocket and pulling the bleeping object out, 'we'll have our special radio-controlled ball back, if you don't mind!'

'Huh?' gasped the Scunner. 'A golf ball? Is that all? Is that what all the fuss was about?'

Super Gran and company walked back up the hill from the riverbank and as the Scunner followed them, with Tub, he patted his right-hand pocket and whispered:

'She had me worried there for a minute, Tub. But they're all right, the diamonds are still safe ...'

'What was that, you wee bachle? Diamonds, did you say?'

Her Super-hearing had picked up the whisper and she spun round, grabbed the Scunner, put her hand into his right-hand pocket and pulled out the bag.

'Curses! Gimme that ...!' The Scunner tried to snatch it back, but she thrust it behind her back.

'So that's what you've been up to! Stealing diamonds!'

'Grrr!' roared the Scunner, angry at being robbed of his ill-gotten gains.

He looked round, spotted the tipped-up buggy with a bag of clubs spilling out of it, grabbed a driver and held it threateningly over Super Gran's head.

'Look, Uncle,' Tub blurted out, pointing skywards again, 'it's going to make its drop ...'

'Quiet, Tub, you fool,' the Scunner said, without looking up.

'So that's how you're getting them, is it?' Super Gran said.

'I don't know what you're talking about,' the Scunner fibbed, still not looking up.

But he was the only one who wasn't looking up, for everyone else's eyes were glued to the model plane as it swooped lower, towards them.

'Look out, Scunner!'

Super Gran pointed upwards but the Scunner ignored her. He was concentrating on clobbering her with the golf club, and nothing was going to distract him!

'Look out, nothing!' he snarled. 'I'm going to clobber you, you interfering old pest. And I'm going to get my diamonds ...'

He got the diamonds all right – the bag fell from the plane and struck him on the head! He went cross-eyed for a second and then crumpled up at Super Gran's feet.

Presently, Willard and Edison were walking away across the golf course, towards the exit, with Super Gran.

'Well, Super Gran,' Edison said, swinging one of the bags of diamonds in her hand, 'you solved a crime you didn't even know had been committed! And you got the diamonds back.'

'Yeah, Gran,' Willard added as he swung the other bag jauntily, 'and you'll probably get a reward, huh?'

Super Gran's hands, resting on her shoulders, were each gripping the handle of a golf club. And the other end of each club was twisted into a loop round the neck of one of her prisoners, the Scunner and Tub, as she led them, trotting along obediently behind her, to Chisleton's 'nick'.

She glanced back over her shoulder and laughed. 'This is just like a game of cards, Scunner. You went for *diamonds* – but I won, with *clubs*!'

Super Gran
and the Double

The door of the poshest jeweller's shop in Chisleton burst
open and the female jewel thief dived inside with a shout:
'This is a haud-up, Jimmy!'

'Pardon?' said Arnold, the shop assistant. 'A hod up? Isn't
that something to do with builders?'

The jewel thief tried again, this time in English! 'This is a
hold-up, James!'

She wore a floral dress, a cardigan and a tartan tammy,
she had a Scottish accent and she appeared to be none other
than Super Gran! And her two accomplices, who had
followed her into the shop, appeared to be none other than
Willard and Edison!

However, on closer inspection, 'Willard', in his football
strip, seemed to be somewhat bigger than usual and had
hairy legs! While 'Edison', also bigger, seemed to be wearing
a wig that was much too large for her! It was the Renta-
Muscles, in disguise, and they were assisting 'Super Gran',
better known as Greta Gorbals, a well-known criminal from
Glasgow.

Arnold put his hands up with a cry of 'Oooh, Mummy,
help!', while 'Super Gran' banged her fist on the glass
counter, which terrified him even more, and said:

'Gie's the rocks, Jock, or it'll be the worse for you!'

Arnold, whose knees were knocking, looked from 'Super
Gran' to 'Willard' and 'Edison'. He couldn't believe his eyes.

'S-Super Gran?' he stuttered.

'Aye, that's right, Jimmy,' said 'Super Gran' in a rough, rasping voice, lifting a bag on to the counter. 'Gie's a' yir jew'lery. Stick it in here!'

'W-Willard? E-E-Edison?' he stammered.

'Move!' said the Renta-Muscle, alias 'Willard'.

Arnold moved. He stuffed all the jewellery he could grab out of the glass counter into the bag. It was wiser not to argue.

'Super Gran', 'Willard' and 'Edison' ran out of the shop.

Their next call was at Chisleton Post Office.

'Hand ower yir pension books!' 'Super Gran' commanded roughly, and 'Willard' and 'Edison' moved along a line of Oldies, grabbing the books out of their hands.

Then 'Super Gran' went over to the counter and barked at the counter clerk, Penny Pinchpenny: 'Hey, you – fish-face! Cash this loat, wull ye? An' be quick aboot it!'

Penny put her hand to her mouth in astonishment. She couldn't believe that Super Gran was behaving like a common criminal.

'But – Super Gran . . . ?' she murmured.

'Aye, it's me – Super Gran. Hoots mon and awa' the noo!'

It didn't *sound* like Super Gran, Penny thought. It sounded more like a bad English imitator! But it certainly *looked* like Super Gran!

As the thieves made their getaway, running along the street, they pushed shoppers aside and 'Super Gran', for devilment, pulled a painter's ladder away from him while he was up it, painting a second-storey window. They all laughed as the man slid down the ladder and landed with a howl in a paint pot. Then, to complete the 'fun', 'Super Gran'

pushed a traffic warden into a hole which workmen were digging in the road!

Presently, word about 'Super Gran's' exploits reached the ears of the Chisleton Police Force.

'I can't understand it,' said PC Leekie, shaking his head, 'it's just not like her to be doing all the rotten, crooked things she's doing.'

'I agree,' his senior officer, Inspector Muggins, replied, 'but we've no alternative, we'll have to bring her in! There are too many reports about her, and they can't *all* be wrong. First the jeweller's, then the Post Office. Come on, let's fetch her.'

A few minutes later Willard – the real one, this time! – was opening his Gran's front door in answer to the persistent knocking of the police. But he had no sooner said 'PC Leekie ...?' than the constable, closely followed by the Inspector, came barging in without waiting for a proper invitation.

'Where is she?' Leekie demanded and then, without waiting to be told, he followed his nose and went crashing through into the kitchen, where Super Gran was baking.

But unfortunately for him, he barged in just as she was bringing a tray of scones out of the oven. He collided with the tray and one of the hot scones popped into his mouth!

'Super Gran,' he began, 'we're here to arr ... ah ... ah ... oh ... ow ... ooyah ...!'

He leapt about with the scone in his mouth, then juggled it about, from mouth to hand and back again, before finally spitting it out. Then he fanned his mouth cool with his hands and rushed to the tap for a handful of cold water to soothe his burned mouth.

'Rupert Leekie! What's going on?' said Super Gran indignantly. 'If you wanted a scone why couldn't you have waited till they cooled? I know my scones are good, but surely you're

not that desperate for one that you –' she glanced up and saw
the Inspector at the door '– that both of you had to come
bursting in here like that, huh?' She frowned, annoyed.

But she was even more annoyed when Muggins said:

'Come off it, Super Gran. Don't come the innocent with us!'

'What d'you mean, Inspector?'

Leekie's mouth had cooled sufficiently for him to be able
to whip his handcuffs out of his pocket and snap them on to
the unsuspecting Super Gran's wrists.

'Hey, what's going on? What d'you think you're doing,
Rupert Leekie?'

'Sorry, Super Gran,' Leekie muttered.

'Hey, what're you doing to my Gran?' demanded Willard from the open kitchen door.

'Have you gone mad, Leekie? And you, Inspector?' she asked.

'No, Super Gran,' the Inspector replied, 'but I think you have! Robbing the jewellery shop, and the Post Office ...'

'What? Me? Robbing? You're joking!'

'We've got eyewitnesses,' Muggins assured her. 'The assistant from the jeweller's shop, the Post Office clerk, the pensioners ...'

Leaving the house, and a puzzled Willard, behind them, they bundled Super Gran into their patrol car and took her to the police station to 'help them with their inquiries'.

'You silly wee bachles,' she kept telling them, all the way there, 'I'm not a crook – I'm Super Gran. You've made a terrible mistake.'

'No, Super Gran,' the Inspector retorted, '*you've* made the mistake – turning crooked!'

Meanwhile, Willard was opening the front door again, to Edison.

'Listen,' she said, 'I've just bumped into Super Gran at the cake shop in town. She looked right through me, as if she didn't know me – then shoved me into a big muddy puddle! Is she ill, or something? What's the matter with her?'

'You *can't* have just seen her,' Willard denied. 'She's been in here all morning, baking. That is, until ...'

'Until what?'

'Until – Leekie and Inspector Muggins arrested her a few minutes ago ...'

'Arrested? Oh no! What for?'

Willard shrugged. 'They say she's robbed a jewellery shop and the Post Office.'

Edison looked thoughtful. 'You know, I wondered about that one in the cake shop. Especially after she kicked my leg and blew me a raspberry! There was something funny about her! I wonder . . .'

'Wonder what?'

'If there are two Super Grans going about . . . ?'

'Two? How could there be?'

'The normal one – and somebody else dressed up as her, going round robbing people and putting the blame on her. It's possible, isn't it?'

'Yeah, but why would anyone want to do that?' Willard asked.

'I dunno,' said Edison, 'but let's go and find out.'

Meanwhile the Scunner was entertaining his guest, Greta Gorbals, who was still dressed as Super Gran. They sat in the Scunner's lounge with Tub, who was leaning towards Greta, offering her a cup of tea.

'And have a sandwich, Greta,' the Scunner said, thrusting a plate of super-thick, doorstep-type sandwiches at her.

She took one, smiled at it in anticipation – not for her the normal, dainty, ladylike sandwich! – and stuffed it greedily into her mouth.

'Ta, Scunner. Jist the joab!'

The Scunner watched her, fascinated, as she wolfed her way through the sandwiches in no time. But Tub, whose hand she slapped every time he reached out to get one for himself, was muttering under his breath that he had no chance while that greedy Greta Gorbals guzzled everything in sight.

'What was that?' Greta demanded, glaring angrily at him.

'N - nothing,' stuttered the terrified Tub, 'nothing.'

And while Greta, alias 'Super Gran', was enjoying her food

at the Scunner's house, the real Super Gran, in the detention room of the Chisleton 'nick', was also asking for food.

'I'm starving, Rupert,' she said, 'could you get me a wee snack, d'you think?'

But this was just a ruse on her part!

Leekie had been in the room with her, guarding her, and they had been discussing whether or not she was guilty of the robberies.

'But I'm telling you,' she'd said, 'I'm innocent. Only I can't prove it while I'm being kept prisoner in here.'

Leekie shrugged. 'But I can't let you out to prove it, can I?'

But when she said she was hungry, he couldn't very well let her starve, could he? So he agreed to go along to the canteen and fetch her some tea and sandwiches.

He returned to the detention room to find that the bird – the jailbird! – had flown. The room was empty. The window was open and the bars on it had been forced apart to allow her to escape.

'Heck! I forgot about her Super-strength,' he muttered.

'Didn't I tell you to stay with her, Leekie?' Muggins muttered angrily.

'Sorry, sir. She was hungry, you see . . .'

And somebody else was hungry – Greta Gorbals, who had now progressed from the doorstep sandwiches to six large sausage rolls, which she had eaten in quick succession! The Scunner, meanwhile, was inspecting with a jeweller's eye-glass the diamonds which she, as 'Super Gran', had stolen.

'M'mm, very nice! And worth a small fortune, if I'm any judge.'

'Hey, talkin' aboot judges,' Greta said, spluttering out bits

of sausage roll all over the Scunner, 'mibbe ah'd better make ma getaway afore ah get nicked.'

'There's no need to worry, Greta. The person who'll get the blame is old pest-face – the real Super Gran! She was the one who was seen doing it and there are lots of witnesses who'll testify to that. Tee, hee, hee.' He laughed uproariously. 'And she's languishing behind bars at this very minute!'

'Well, Scunner,' said Greta, cuddling into his arm, 'if ah don't have tae make a quick getaway ah might as well stay here and get ma photy taken.'

'Photy? I mean . . . photo? What photo? What for?'

'Well, ev'ry time ah pull a joab in wan o' ma many disguises ah get ma photy taken, tae send tae the *Gangsters' Gazette*.'

'But that's much too risky, Greta.'

'Why is it? Aw, go oan, let me get ma photy taken in ma "Super Gran" gear. Eh?' She fluttered her eyelashes at him persuasively.

'Oh, all right then,' he agreed. 'We'll go down to the Photo Studio in the High Street. Let's go. You too, Tub.'

Tub grabbed the few crumbs that Greta had left on the plate, then followed them out to the car. A few minutes later it pulled up near the studio and Greta stepped out.

The Scunner leaned out of his window and called after her.

'We'll wait here for you. But be quick about it!'

'A' right, a' right,' she yelled back, 'keep yir sporran oan!'

She entered the studio and pinged the bell on the counter for attention. The shop was full of dust, cobwebs and old photographic equipment and an assistant, Roddy, suddenly popped out from behind the counter.

'Well?' he snapped.

'Aye, ah'm fine thanks, Jimmy,' Greta replied cheerily.

'No,' he corrected, 'I mean – yes?'

'Make up yir mind, son. Which is it – no, or yes?'

The snappy Roddy got even snappier. 'Can I help you?'

'Ah waant ma photy taken. A portrait. Ah waant you to make me look young, beau'iful and glamorous . . .'

Roddy interrupted her in mid-flow. 'I'm a photographer, madam, not a miracle-worker!'

But while the snappy Roddy prepared to take a snapshot of Greta, alias 'Super Gran', the real Super Gran was hurrying along a side street, and she was fuming.

'Humph! So someone's going around impersonating me, are they? Just wait till I get my hands on them!'

She turned the corner into the High Street and walked straight past the Photo Studio. Seconds later the door opened and Greta emerged, clutching a large 'instant' photograph in her hands. She paused to admire it, then stepped into the street and turned left, the opposite direction from that taken by the real Super Gran.

The result of this was that one Super Gran was walking *up* the High Street, while the second one was walking *down* the High Street!

Suddenly a police patrol car appeared, driven by Leekie, with Muggins hanging out of the window, yelling through a loud-hailer.

'Attention! Attention! Be on the look-out for Super Gran, who has escaped from police custody ...'

The Scunner and Tub, sitting in their parked car along the road from the studio, had noticed neither of the Super Grans in the High Street. The Scunner had been too busy reading his *Gangsters' Gazette*, while Tub had been too busy munching a chocolate crunchy and reading the *Beano*!

But they heard the police announcement. They couldn't help hearing it!

'Oh-oh, looks like it's time we scarpered,' the Scunner muttered as he started up the car.

Greta, still admiring her photograph, had almost reached the car when she saw it suddenly roaring off.

'Hey! Scunner, ye wee scunner! Whit're ye playin' at? Wait fur me!'

But he didn't! He drove off, leaving behind a fuming Greta.

Meanwhile, across the street, Willard and Edison thought they were seeing double – which they were! Not only could they see Super Gran passing a greengrocer's shop but they could also see her 'twin', outside the baker's shop, holding a large photograph in one hand while shaking her other fist at the Scunner's departing car.

'Look, Willard ...' Edison pointed.

'You were right, there *are* two Super Grans! And that one over there seems to know the Scunner.'

'Super Gran!' Edison shouted – and both of them turned!

'Which is the real one?' Willard yelled, pointing with both hands to the Super Grans, a few shops apart from each other.

The real Super Gran looked at the phoney one and thought for a moment that she was looking in a mirror! Then she shook her fist at her 'double'.

'You . . . you wee scunnerylugs! What's the idea impersonating me and getting me the blame for all your rotten crimes?'

Super Gran's first impulse was not to run and tackle Greta, but to grab the first thing that came to hand and throw it at her. And, as she was standing outside the greengrocer's, the first thing that came to hand was a large, hard cauliflower. She threw it.

But Greta retaliated.

A delivery man was passing with a board of loaves from his van to the baker's shop just then, so Greta, yelling 'Gie's yir breid, Jimmy!', grabbed the largest, heaviest loaf from it and threw it at Super Gran.

Super Gran dodged the flying loaf and grabbed up an armful of vegetables with which to bombard, and stun, Greta – at about one hundred miles per hour!

But the battle didn't go unnoticed by the police!

'There she is!' cried Leekie, pointing through the windscreen.

'You mean,' Muggins corrected him, 'there they are! There's two of them! Super Gran must've been telling the truth after all!'

'Yeah,' Leekie said, 'but which one's . . . ?'

'... The real one? I dunno,' Muggins confessed, scratching his head, puzzled.

'I know!' cried Leekie. 'We'll make them both do something Super – like lifting a car – and the real one'll be able to do it!'

'Good idea,' Muggins smiled, 'and the fake one won't!'

But they didn't have to put the two Super Grans to the test, for right then they put themselves to the test.

Just as the real Super Gran was dodging the hail of loaves which Greta was throwing at her, she heard, with her Super-hearing, a cry for help.

'That sounds like Penny Pinchpenny,' she said, 'down by the river. Hold on, Super Gran's here. I'm just coming!'

She turned, raced along the High Street, leap-frogged over two small children in passing, then ran down a side street which led to the River Chisle.

And Greta did likewise! She had to, or else she would have given the show away!

'Er ... ah ... um ... Super Gran's here ... Haud oan, hen ... Ah'm jist comin' ...' she yelled.

Then, still clutching her photograph, she ran after the real Super Gran, but when she tried to leap-frog the children she couldn't get over them and just pushed them into a puddle!

And when Greta ran after Super Gran, so did Willard, Edison, Muggins, Leekie, Roddy the photographer – waving a camera about – and just about everyone else who was in the High Street at the time!

The Scunner, on the other hand, was on his way out of the High Street, escaping, when he saw all this commotion. He screeched the car to a halt, jumped out – hauling Tub with him – and ran to join the throng of people chasing after Super Gran.

'Come on, Tub. This I must see.'

'Help!' screeched Penny, from a boat which was sinking lower and lower in the water. 'Can't you do something, Arnold?' she asked her boyfriend, the jeweller's assistant. 'I thought you knew all about rowing!'

By now she was baling out the water with her bare hands, but not too successfully!

'Well, I watch the Boat Race every year,' Arnold informed her, as if that made him an expert!

Just then, as the boat had almost filled with water, Super Gran arrived on the scene. Which was just as well, for the boat was not only sinking, it was also heading towards a fast-flowing weir a few metres away.

'Have no fear, Super Gran's here . . .' she yelled to Penny and Arnold.

Behind her, Greta, Muggins, Leekie, Willard, Edison, Roddy – still waving his camera about – the Scunner, Tub and everyone else from the High Street had arrived to watch the rescue.

Super Gran dived from the riverbank and swam towards the boat. By now it was completely under water and Penny and Arnold, while trying to keep themselves afloat, were looking worriedly at the rapidly approaching weir.

'Got you!' said Super Gran as she grabbed them.

But then she had to fight to keep all three of them away from the weir's strong currents.

Turning over on to her back so that she could put her arms round Penny and Arnold, she swam back towards the shore. At the riverbank, Leekie and Muggins ran forward to haul the three of them out.

'You saved us, Super Gran,' cried Penny.

'Yes, you sure did,' Arnold added.

'Och, it was nothing, folks,' she said modestly.

And while everyone on the riverbank had been watching this drama, snap-happy Roddy had been snapping away with his camera. But he didn't just photograph the rescue, he also took shots of all the spectators who were watching it, open-mouthed – Muggins, Leekie, Greta, Willard, Edison and everyone else who had come along from the High Street. The exceptions to this, of course, were the Scunner and Tub, who were skulking about in the background.

But now everyone turned their attention towards Greta, the phoney 'Super Gran', who stood in the centre of the crowd.

'Come on, then,' Muggins challenged her, 'let's see *you* do something super, if you're really Super Gran . .'

'Yeah, come on ...'

'Go ahead – do something super ...' everyone urged her.

'Yeah, go on,' echoed Tub, going forward from where he and the Scunner were skulking.

The Scunner yanked him back. 'Not you, Tub. You know she can't do anything super, you idiot!'

'Oh, yeah, you're right,' Tub admitted sheepishly. 'I forgot!'

'A' right,' said Greta, in the centre of the angry mob, 'ah give up. Ah admit ah'm no the real Super Gran. OK?' She held her wrists out to receive Leekie's handcuffs. 'Ah'm really Greta Gorbals, if ye must know.'

'What? The famous Glasgow gangster and mistress of disguise?' gasped Muggins.

'Aye,' she replied, and pointed with her handcuffed hands at Leekie. 'An' dis guy's goat me! It's a fair cop, so it is!'

The Scunner sidled up to her and muttered out of the corner of his mouth: 'Huh! You and your blinkin' photos!'

'And talking of photos,' said Roddy, who'd had his best day's business for months, snapping away at everyone in sight for the last ten minutes, 'these will all be ready, first thing tomorrow morning – at a reasonable price.'

Meanwhile Super Gran was speaking to Muggins.

'Inspector, I've just been reading Greta's mind and I think she's got something to tell you – about her accomplices. They were disguised as Willard and Edison, I believe ...'

'What?' said Willard and Edison, looking at each other.

'Not to mention,' Super Gran went on, 'the person she passed the stolen jewellery on to. The Scunner – who else?'

Muggins swung round on the Scunner as he tried to slope off and mingle with the crowd. 'Scunner ...?'

The Scunner reached into his pocket and whipped out a diamond bracelet. 'Perhaps a small token of my regard – for your dear lady wife . . . ? No? Oh well, perhaps not.'

Muggins snapped a pair of handcuffs on him, then grabbed – and handcuffed – Tub, who was also trying to slip away and merge into the crowd.

Leekie put his arm round Super Gran's shoulders and gave her a hug. 'Sorry about the misunderstanding, Super Gran,' he apologized.

'Och, don't worry about it, laddie, these things happen.'

'Tell you what,' he went on, 'just to show there's no hard feelings, why don't we make use of Roddy and his camera and have a photograph taken? Of all of us?'

'Good idea,' she said, as they all clustered around her, smiled and said 'Cheese!'

There was Super Gran, Willard, Edison, Leekie, Muggins, Penny, Arnold and just about everyone else from the High Street all staring at the camera. But of course the Scunner, Tub and Greta Gorbals were not invited to be in it! They would have their own photograph taken, later, for the *Gangsters' Gazette*!

'I can't quite get you all in,' said Roddy. 'Can you move back a bit?'

'There's no room,' said Super Gran. '*You* move back a bit.'
He did.

'I'm *still* not getting you all in,' he complained.

'Then move back a bit farther,' Super Gran suggested.
He did.

There was a loud splash.

'Oh-oh, here we go again,' said Super Gran, as she ran forward to rescue Roddy from the river. 'There's never a dull moment when I'm around, is there . . . ?'

Super Gran
and the Dognappers

Super Gran and Willard were having a nice quiet day at the seaside, at Paddleton-on-Sea. At least, that's what Willard had been hoping for – but nice quiet days and Super Gran just didn't seem to go together!

All that Willard wanted to do was to lie about on the beach, go paddling, have a kick-about with his football on the sand and eat a few ice lollies. Nothing too strenuous. But that wasn't quite how it turned out!

'Now remember, Gran,' he kept saying, 'you agreed that we'd just have a nice quiet day at the seaside! No climbing multi-storey buildings to rescue cats or lifting buses or anything! Just a quiet day out, right?'

'Jings! Who wants to have a quiet day out?' asked Super Gran, as she leapt over a large pile of deckchairs on the prom!

She then jumped up on the promenade wall and raced along it until she came to a gap – which she leapt across!

Willard shrugged and shook his head. What was the use? His Gran just didn't seem to be capable of having a nice quiet day out.

Then she spotted the water-bikes!

These were motorcycles which were driven at speed through the waves, and they were for hire from a little jetty down on the beach.

'Oh, look!' she said, pointing. 'I fancy a wee shot on one of those!'

'Gran!' said Willard.

'Och, all right,' she promised, as they went down on to the sand, 'we'll have a nice quiet day at the seaside for once, and we'll just lie about on the beach and sunbathe, eh?'

So they did that – for a little while!

'They say,' she said, 'that nothing ever happens here in Paddleton-on-Sea. It's a one-horse town. Or rather,' she laughed, pointing to the animal plodding up and down the beach with a child on its back, 'it's a one-donkey town! So we're bound to have a quiet day here, aren't we?'

But she spoke too soon, for on the cliffs nearby, sitting in a seaside shelter, were the Scunner and Tub!

The Scunner kept glancing over the top of the *Gangsters' Gazette*, which he was reading, while Tub glanced over the

top of the *Dandy*! They were awaiting the arrival of their latest victim, although Tub wasn't too sure who that was.

'Who are we waiting for, Uncle, huh?'

'We're waiting for Glad, that's who.'

'Who's Glad?' asked Tub.

'I am – glad we're not in prison!' the Scunner chortled as Tub scowled. 'No, I'm only joking. I really meant Glad – Gladys – Gladys Grocklebank.'

'Who's Gladys Grocklebank?' Tub asked.

'She's . . .' began the Scunner, then stopped. 'Shhhh! Here she comes . . .'

Tub peeked out of the shelter from behind his *Dandy*, and spotted a stout woman with a huge dog on a lead. The dog's name was Darlikins and it was wearing on its neck, hanging from its collar, a little barrel, in imitation of the ones carried by St Bernard dogs in the mountains.

'Here, take this,' the Scunner whispered, handing Tub a large net. 'You know what to do . . .?'

'Yeah,' said Tub as he took the net and put down his *Dandy* on the seat of the shelter.

He advanced on Gladys and the dog, but Gladys, right at the edge of the cliff, gave a scream.

Down on the beach, along from the foot of the cliff, Super Gran jumped to her feet. 'Jings! That sounds like a cry for help!'

'Oh no,' Willard groaned, 'you promised! A nice quiet day at the seaside?' They hadn't even managed to get a kick-about with his football yet!

'It can't be helped, laddie,' she said. 'If someone's in danger I'll have to help them.' And she ran across the sand towards the cliff.

At the top of the cliff, Gladys was sniffling into a large, lacy, scented handkerchief as she looked downwards over the edge. 'Oh, my poor Darlikins . . .'

When Tub had approached the dog with the net, it had turned to growl at him, but missed its footing and slipped over the edge, sliding down a slippery slope and ending up on a narrow ledge, halfway down the cliff-face.

'Help!' shrieked Gladys, and:

'Oo-er!' gasped Tub as he ran from the scene of the crime to the shelter in the distance.

But help was at hand. Two policemen patrolling the cliff-top appeared on the scene and offered to rescue Darlikins. Or at least, one of them, Sergeant Sergeant, offered that the other one, Constable Constable, would rescue Darlikins!

And so, below Gladys's feet, Sergeant Sergeant of the local police force was helping the terrified Constable Constable down the slope, holding his arm.

'Hurry!' Gladys cried. 'My poor Darlikins is trapped down there.'

'Yes, we can see that, madam,' Sergeant said, 'and we *are* hurrying. Down you go, Constable.'

'Yes, but why me, Sarge?' Constable moaned, looking down at the sea, hundreds of metres below.

'Because I'm a sergeant,' said Sergeant Sergeant, 'and you're just a constable, Constable Constable!'

Below them on the ledge, growling viciously, stood Darlikins. While below Darlikins, at the foot of the cliff, stood Super Gran.

She put her hands round her mouth and, using a Super-breath, shouted up to them. 'Can I help you?'

'What – you? A little old lady?' Sergeant yelled back, as he and Constable looked down the slope. 'Don't be ridiculous! Just leave this to hefty he-men, OK?'

'Well ... ah ... um ... if you really want to help ...' began Constable, starting to come up the slippery slope again.

'Oh, no you don't, Constable Constable. Get on with it,' Sergeant Sergeant ordered.

So Constable had to continue downwards, until he was beginning to get dangerously close to Darlikins' growling jaws.

'My poor little Darlikins!' Gladys screamed suddenly. 'Save him, somebody! Hurry up!'

'I'm telling you, we *are* hurrying,' Sergeant assured her, a trifle shortly, adding: 'Hurry up, Constable ...'

'It's all right for *you*!' muttered Constable under his breath, 'but I'm the one down here trying to rescue this great lump of mutt!'

By this time he was farther down the slope towards the ledge, and had had to let go of the sergeant's hand. It was all highly dangerous, and he looked down at the rocks below and gulped.

But below him Super Gran was taking matters into her own hands. She was going to help with the rescue whether the police sergeant liked it or not!

She looked round and spotted a boat nearby, with a long rope and anchor attached to it.

'The very thing!' she cried as she ran to it, unfastened the rope, hauled the anchor out of the sand and ran back to the foot of the cliff with it.

Then, holding the rope and twirling the anchor above her head like a huge South American bolas, she shouted, 'Look out, up there!' then she let go of the anchor, aiming it at the top of the cliff, where it landed with a loud 'clunk'.

Making sure that the anchor was firmly embedded in the grass at the cliff-top, she quickly climbed the rope, hand over hand, up the cliff-face. Gladys, Sergeant and Constable could only stare over the edge of the cliff at her, open-mouthed with amazement.

In no time at all she had reached the ledge, tucked Darli-kins under her arm and continued upwards to Gladys and Sergeant on the cliff-top. She handed the dog back to its grateful mistress, whose tears of happiness were splashing all over it!

'Oh, my little doggie is safe once more,' she cried.

Constable Constable, halfway down the slope, had mixed feelings about the rescue. On the one hand he was relieved that he didn't have to proceed any farther down the cliff-face to face the growling dog. But at the same time there was a sense of having failed – and having been shamed by a little old lady!

'But how did it get down there?' Super Gran asked Gladys. 'Did it fall?'

'My poor boy was being chased along the cliff by a tubby little youth who went for him with a big net, as if he was going to kidnap him. "Come to Tub," he said ...'

'Tub?' gasped Super Gran. 'Surely not? Here in Paddle-ton?'

'Do you know him?' Sergeant asked, but he was inter-rupted by a cry from the slope below them.

'Never mind that, Sarge,' Constable yelled, 'get me up out of here!'

'Oh, I'd forgotten about Constable!' said Sergeant as he looked over the cliff-edge. 'Can't you get up by yourself lad?'

'Here, I'll get him,' said Super Gran, pushing Sergeant aside.

She plunged down the slope far enough to grab Constable's

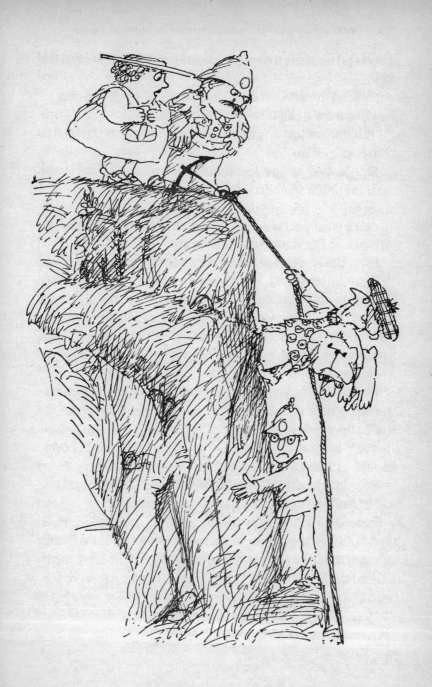

hand and haul the trembling, shaking policeman back to the top.

'Whew!' he said. 'Thanks. But I never thought I'd ever be rescued from a cliff-face by a little old lady!'

'But I'm not just any little old lady,' Super Gran explained, 'I'm Super Gran!'

She looked at the less-than-immaculate Constable. By now his uniform was covered in twigs, moss and grass – and a seagull was perched on his shoulder!

'It's a good job I was here, wasn't it?' she said to Sergeant. 'To rescue Darlikins – and your constable?'

'Er . . . um . . . yes, I . . . um . . . suppose so . . .' Sergeant said.

'Sometimes you big, strong, hefty he-men need a frail little old lady to help you, don't you?' she went on.

'Er . . . um . . . yes, yes, I suppose so,' Sergeant admitted.

Meanwhile, in the shelter farther along the cliff, the Scunner and Tub had been watching the rescue from a safe distance.

'Curses! Trust that pest Super Gran to show up! But what's she doing here in Paddleton? And just as we were about to snaffle the mutt, too!'

'Yeah, but it wasn't my fault that the stupid thing fell over the cliff as I was about to catch it.'

'Bungling bananas!' the Scunner cursed. 'So near and yet so far. And the mutt's our passport to a fortune.'

Some time later Gladys was lounging contentedly in a deckchair on the prom, with her darling Darlikins lying snoozing beside her, tied to the chair. But neither of them noticed the Scunner and Tub creeping up on them from the rear.

'Here, doggy! Nice doggy . . . !' said the Scunner, putting his hand out towards it.

Darlikins opened his eyes, growled and showed the Scunner what large teeth he had! All the better to bite him with!

Unnoticed by Gladys, the villains crept closer to the deck-chair and made a grab at the dog. But the dog, in turn, made a dive at them. The result was that its lead pulled at the deckchair, which collapsed, throwing Gladys on to the prom in a heap.

'Help!' she screamed.

The Scunner and Tub made a run for it and dodged behind an ice-cream kiosk to hide.

While Gladys was scrambling to her feet, Sergeant Sergeant and Constable Constable passed along the prom on their beat. She appealed to them:

'Sergeant, I'm telling you, someone is trying to steal my Darlikins ...'

'I see, madam,' said Sergeant. 'Tell me, is Darlikins a Crufts champion? Or is he a very rare breed? Or does he have false teeth made from emeralds, perhaps?'

'No, no, no,' replied Gladys, in answer to his three questions, 'but I still say that someone's ...'

She was interrupted by a growl, as Darlikins tried to persuade Sergeant and Constable to believe his mistress's story. And also to demonstrate that his teeth were very real, and very sharp!

'But why should anyone want to steal this ... this :..' Sergeant began. Darlikins growled at him again. 'This ... this dear little doggie?'

He tried to smile a sweet smile at the big, vicious-looking brute as he fibbed!

'That's what I don't know,' Gladys said.

'Oh well,' Sergeant shrugged, as he and Constable plodded off, 'that's it, then.'

Nearby, the Scunner and Tub were skulking about behind the ice-cream kiosk, while Tub licked an ice lolly.

'But what's so special about that horrible mutt, Uncle?' he asked, between slurps.

'The horrible mutt used to belong to Grizzly Grocklebank.'

'The safe-breaker?' gasped Tub.

'Whose haul from his last job was never found,' the Scunner went on. 'But one night in prison he talked in his sleep and gave away the hiding place of something that would lead to the loot.'

'And the dog's got it?'

The Scunner nodded. 'Quiet, Tub – here comes Super Gran ...'

She and Willard arrived at the kiosk to buy the boy his fifth ice lolly of the morning! Then they went over to speak to Gladys.

'He's such a lovely, darling boy,' said Gladys, as she bent to pat Darlikins. 'But why should anyone want to steal him, Super Gran?'

Willard thought to himself that 'lovely, darling boy' was hardly the way he would have described the brute!

'Maybe it's not the dog itself they're after,' Super Gran said. 'Maybe it's something . . .'

She stopped. She had suddenly spotted the little barrel round Darlikins' neck. She aimed her X-ray vision at it.

'Aha!' she cried.

'What is it, Super Gran?' Gladys asked.

'Don't tell me the Crown Jewels are in there?' Willard giggled, between licks at his lolly.

Super Gran took the barrel off the dog's collar and handed it to Gladys to open.

'It's a photo,' said Gladys, 'all rolled up.' She showed it to Super Gran.

'Just a wee photo? Of a beach hut?' she said, puzzled.

Gladys took the photo back and looked at it. 'But this is the one that my late husband and I used to use, here in Paddleton.' She turned it over. 'See, its location's written on the back – Row H, Block 3, Hut 4.'

But she had been overheard by the Scunner and Tub, who were now skulking even nearer, behind a souvenir kiosk.

'That's it, Tub. That's where the loot's hidden,' cried the Scunner in triumph.

But if the Scunner understood all about the beach hut and its secret, Super Gran certainly didn't.

'What's it all about, Gladys?' she asked. 'And why is there

a photo of a beach hut inside a barrel round a dog's neck?'

'Come on,' Gladys said, by way of an answer, 'I must contact the police again. I'll tell you all about it on the way ...'

But the sergeant still wasn't interested.

He was off duty and had been waiting at a café table on the prom, with his helmet off, while Constable fetched their tea and sandwiches from the self-service counter. He had been looking forward to a little bit of a rest when the stout Gladys hove into sight once again, not only with the large, horrible Darlikins on its lead, but also with Super Gran and Willard in tow.

'Oh no,' he groaned, 'not again! What is it this time?'

He was showing no sign of interest, so Gladys decided she would just have to tell him who she was.

'Maybe you'll listen to me, Sergeant, when I explain that I'm the widow of Grizzly Grocklebank ...'

'The safe-breaker ... ?'

He jumped to his feet all excited, knocking over his chair, as Constable arrived at the table with the tea and sandwiches.

'Constable, put your helmet on, quickly!'

'But Sarge, the tea ...'

'Your helmet!' Sergeant snapped.

'But I'm starving, Sarge ...'

'Constable Constable!'

'Yes, Sergeant Sergeant!'

They ran from the café and jumped on to a beach bicycle parked nearby. But the trouble was it was a side-by-side tandem and they couldn't agree which way to go, so some time was lost while they argued about it!

Meanwhile, creeping around the rows of beach huts, look-

ing for the correct one, farther along the beach, were the Scunner and Tub.

'Block H, Row 4, Hut 3,' the Scunner kept muttering over and over again, so that he wouldn't forget it.

'No, Uncle, it was Row H, Block 3, Hut 4,' said Tub.

'Don't confuse me, Tub. Here it is ...'

The Scunner opened the door – and a woman inside screamed!

'Oh, sorry madam – wrong hut ...!'

He moved farther along the beach to another hut where Tub stood waiting, a huge grin on his face.

'This is it, Uncle. Didn't I tell you?'

'All right, all right, don't go on so.' The Scunner bent to pick the lock.

The door swung open and they rushed inside, to find a large heavy wooden chest in a corner, with 'The property of Grizzly Grocklebank' scratched on a metal plate on it.

'Eureka!' the Scunner cried in triumph as he examined it. 'The loot! It's all mine! I'm rich!'

But the Scunner's exploits had been spotted at long distance by Super Gran on the prom.

The sergeant had had the bright idea of jumping off the bike and having a look through the money-in-the-slot telescope on the prom, to see if anything was happening along at the beach huts. But it hadn't been too successful. To begin with, none of them had any small change for it and then, when they finally managed to borrow a coin from a passerby – the telescope wasn't working anyway!

But while Sergeant and Constable had been fiddling about with the telescope, Super Gran had been busy. She merely stood on the prom and directed her Super-eyesight towards the huts at the far end of the beach.

'It *is* the Scunner,' she said, 'I thought it must be him. And Tub. And they've just gone into a hut, so *that* must be the one.'

Gladys turned to the sergeant. 'You're not going to let them get away with my Grizzly's loot, are you?'

Sergeant climbed on to the beach bike again. 'Certainly not, madam. Paddleton-on-Sea's Flying Squad is about to go into action! Come on, Constable, climb aboard. On yer bike!'

But Super Gran yelled after them, 'They're making a run for it! Towards the harbour! I'll go this way and cut them off!' She pointed seawards.

'What way?' asked Willard, puzzled.

But she wasn't there to reply. She had jumped down from the prom, raced across the sand and leapt on to one of the water-bikes which were for hire – only she wasn't going to pay for the ride!

'And I was only saying a wee while ago that I fancied a wee shot on this!' she said, as she started it up.

'Hey! Lady!' yelled the man in charge. 'Stop! Come back!'

'I just want a wee loan of it,' she explained. 'I'm part of Paddleton-on-Sea's Flying Squad! Honestly! I'm the "sea" part of it! I'm the water police!'

She zoomed the bike away across the water before the man could do anything but shake his fist at her retreating figure.

Meanwhile the Scunner and Tub were struggling along the beach from the huts, carrying Grizzly's chest of loot towards the harbour. Each of them held one of its handles, but even so it was heavy. And behind them, as they ran, they could hear Paddleton Flying Squad's equivalent of a police-car siren – two tinkling bicycle bells!

The Scunner glanced round and saw that neither man could steer the bike properly. In fact, it was out of control! The bike wobbled about a bit and then headed towards some coils of rope piled up on the prom. It hit them and the policemen were catapulted over the handlebars to land up, dazed, against a large litter bin.

'Ow! Ouch!' they yelled.

'They're just *rubbish*!' the Scunner laughed, adding: 'Come on, Tub, I've got a speed boat waiting at the end of the jetty.'

'A speed boat?' gasped Tub when he saw it.

'Well, it's got an outboard motor, what more do you want? Come on, get in.'

They jumped aboard, lowered the chest in, started up the motor and set off. But before they had gone a dozen metres there was a yell from behind them.

'Hey! Scunner! Yoo-hoo!' It was Super Gran on her speeding water-bike.

'Oh no!' said Tub, glancing over his shoulder.

'Ye gods and little tartan fishes,' cursed the Scunner as he too spotted her. 'That woman gets everywhere. She's a menace.'

She was rapidly catching up with them and as she got nearer and nearer the Scunner kept looking back to see just how near she was. But the trouble was, Tub was looking back too. Which meant that no one was looking forward! So no one saw the harbour wall looming large, ahead of them!

'Look out, Uncle!' Tub yelled, as he suddenly looked ahead and saw it. But too late!

'What is it, Tub . . . ? Oh no!' said the Scunner, as the boat smashed itself to pieces against the wall.

Super Gran helped to fish them out of the water and up on to the jetty, to be received by Sergeant Sergeant and Constable Constable, who had picked themselves out of the litter bin and run round the harbour to the Scunner's shipwreck!

Then Super Gran, using a fisherman's large net, managed to catch the chest, which had floated away, and pull it ashore like a trawlerman hauling aboard a catch of herring.

'There you are, Sergeant,' she said, presenting him with the chest. 'That's the Scunner and Tub caught and the loot recovered.'

'Thanks, Super Gran,' he said.

By now Willard and Gladys, with Darlikins on its lead, had run round from the prom to the harbour to join them.

'Oh, great!' cried Gladys. 'You've got Grizzly's loot back.' She smiled. 'That'll keep me going till I get the old-age pension.'

'Ah, not so fast, madam,' Sergeant Sergeant said, taking out his notebook and pencil and writing notes. 'This loot doesn't belong to you ...'

'What?' cried Gladys. 'But – but ...'

'Oh no, madam,' he went on, taking great pleasure in it. 'This loot is stolen property, after all, and must be handed back to its rightful owner. I'm afraid we must confiscate it, see?' Then he smiled. 'But the chest seems to have belonged to your hubby – so you'll be able to claim that!'

'*Chest* so!' muttered Gladys. 'Oh well, easy come, easy go. And I've always got my little Darlikins, haven't I?' She smiled down at the anything-but-little dog.

Super Gran put her arm around Willard's shoulder as they walked away from the harbour.

'And *I've* always got my little darlingkins, haven't I, Willie, dear?' she grinned.

'Hoi! Give over, Gran,' said Willard, embarrassed, as he wriggled out of his Gran's embrace. 'But at least that's all the excitement over and we can go back to having a nice quiet day out at the seaside, huh, Gran?'

They both laughed.